For Joni and Pearl

First published 2023 by Walker Books Ltd, 87 Vauxhall Walk, London SE11 5HJ

2 4 6 8 10 9 7 5 3 1

© 2023 Catherine Rayner

The right of Catherine Rayner to be identified as author of this work has been asserted
in accordance with the Copyright, Designs and Patents Act 1988

This book has been typeset in Baskerville MT

Printed in China

British Library Cataloguing in Publication Data: a catalogue record for this book
is available from the British Library

ISBN 978-1-5295-0153-7

www.walker.co.uk

WALKER BOOKS
AND SUBSIDIARIES
LONDON · BOSTON · SYDNEY · AUCKLAND

Molly, Olive & Dexter

Catherine Rayner

At the bottom of the garden, there's an oak tree.

It's home to Molly the hare, Olive the owl and Dexter the fox.

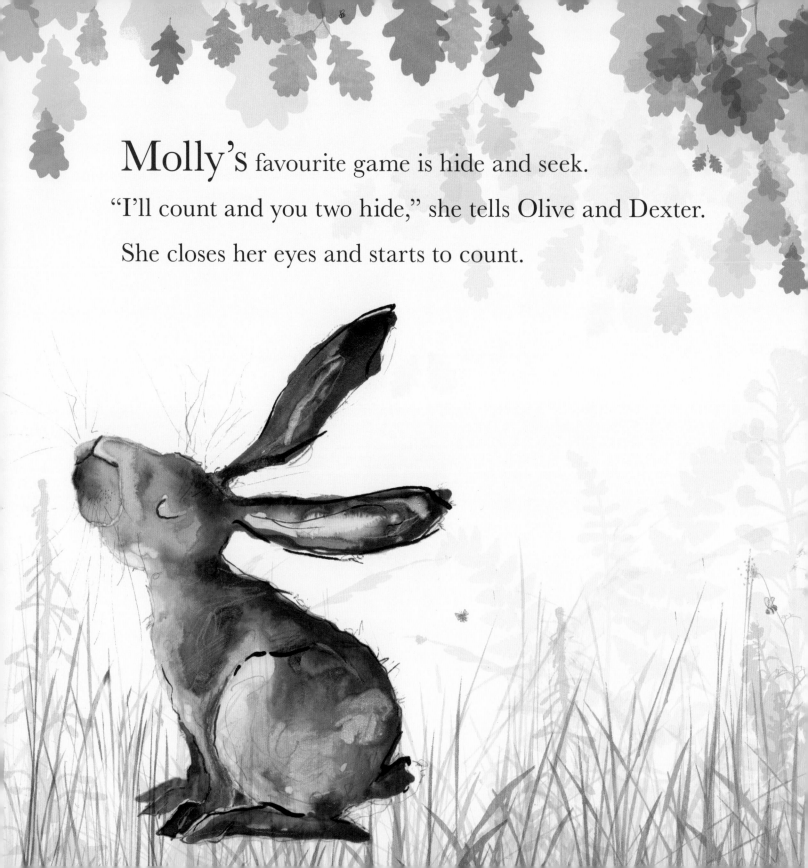

Molly's favourite game is hide and seek.

"I'll count and you two hide," she tells Olive and Dexter.

She closes her eyes and starts to count.

"5, 4, 3, 2 … 1!

Ready or not, here I come."

Molly looks around – and Olive

and Dexter are right there!

"You're supposed to **HIDE**,"

she tells them.

"But we are," says Olive,
  still hiding behind her wings.

"That's right," says Dexter.

"We can't even see you, Molly."

"But *I* can see *you*." Molly thumps the ground with her big foot. "You're supposed to find a place to hide."

"That sounds like fun," says Dexter. "Let's try again."

Molly closes her eyes and starts to count:
"5, 4, 3, 2 ... 1! Ready or not, here I come."

She looks behind the tree…

There they are!

"Olive and Dexter, you're supposed
to **HIDE**," she tells them.

"But we ARE," says Dexter.

"We couldn't see you at all."

"You need to play properly," says Molly firmly. "Go away and really hide."

"All right, Molly!" Olive hoots.

"Let's try again."

Molly closes her eyes and starts to count:

"5, 4, 3, 2 … 1!

Ready or not, here I come."

She looks around, and …

Molly is all alone.

She can't see Olive or Dexter anywhere.

She looks behind
the oak tree –
no, not there.

She hops through
the foxgloves –
no, not there.

She looks over the
big garden wall –
no, not there.

She even peers into the pile of logs,
just in case …

but there's still no
sign of her friends.

Now it seems like her friends have been gone for AGES.

"They must be far, far away," she tells herself.

"What if they got lost when I told them to hide?

I'll never see them again and it's all my fault."

Poor, poor Molly.

But then Molly hears something:
first, a rustle … then a swooping
sound … and was that a hoot?
She looks around, and…

There are OLIVE and
DEXTER, landing on the
ground right beside her.
"Oh, Olive! Oh, Dexter!"
cries Molly. "You've come
back from far, far away!"

"Far, far away?" says Olive, puzzled.
"We never really went anywhere!"
"But you weren't behind the tree," says
Molly, "or in the flowerbed, or anywhere
in the garden. Where *were* you?"

Olive and Dexter start to laugh.
"We were up in the tree the
WHOLE TIME!" they tell her.

Molly laughs too, and Olive puts a soft wing around her.

"You don't have to worry, Molly," she says.

"We'll **NEVER** go far, far away."

And before long they settle under the oak tree
at the bottom of the garden for a nice long nap.

Three best friends.